THE FASCINATING HISTORY OF ASTRONOMY

Published by Westminster Junior Primary School Westminster, Western Australia

Copyright © 2016

Book Design by Judith Price

ISBN 978-0-9954086-1-6

THE FASCINATING HISTORY OF ASTRONOMY

Told by the children in year 2 and 3 Room 4
Westminster Junior Primary School Western Australia

Contents

Written and illustrated by

Adam Yassin Adly Aly
Joseph Boiluh
Tyson Bunter-Pilbeam
Kody Comley
Kahliyah Dempster
Mary Fiel
Tyren Georgiou
Edward Harris
Elijah Headland
Jack Hill
Carol Lako
Anthony Laku
Layan Mousa
Ollie O'Donoghue
Mark Pickett
Ashleigh Smith
Maletia Stack
Hilina Gizat Tegegne
Zion Tukiri
Richard Winemalei
Adam Yappo

Foreword

We children have always looked up at the night sky and wondered about those beautiful twinkling stars, lighting up the sky. When we were just little kids, we learnt to sing nursery rhymes such as Twinkle Twinkle Little Star and Hey Diddle Diddle where the cow jumps over the Moon and many other nice songs about space. We became so fascinated by those twinkling stars; we decided to find out more and write a book for children to read, about the fascinating history of astronomy.

This delightful book written and illustrated by young children is a real treasure. Providing an easy-to-read introduction to general astronomy, it also acknowledges the ancient and enduring origins of Australian Aboriginal astronomy. The book describes how Aboriginal people read the signs of the heavens, when to harvest food sources, how the Sun and Moon are linked to tides and explains eclipses of the Sun and the Moon. Dreamtime stories of the Sun, Moon and constellations are also included. This book should be in every library around Australia.

Len Yarren and Shane Garlett
WADJAK Northside Aboriginal Community Group

What is astronomy?

Astronomy is the study of the universe.

Have people always known about astronomy?

People have always been fascinated about the universe. The people who study it are called astronomers.

What is the universe?

The universe is the collection of all things that exist in space. It is made of millions of stars, galaxies, solar systems, and enormous clouds of gas, separated by gigantic empty space.

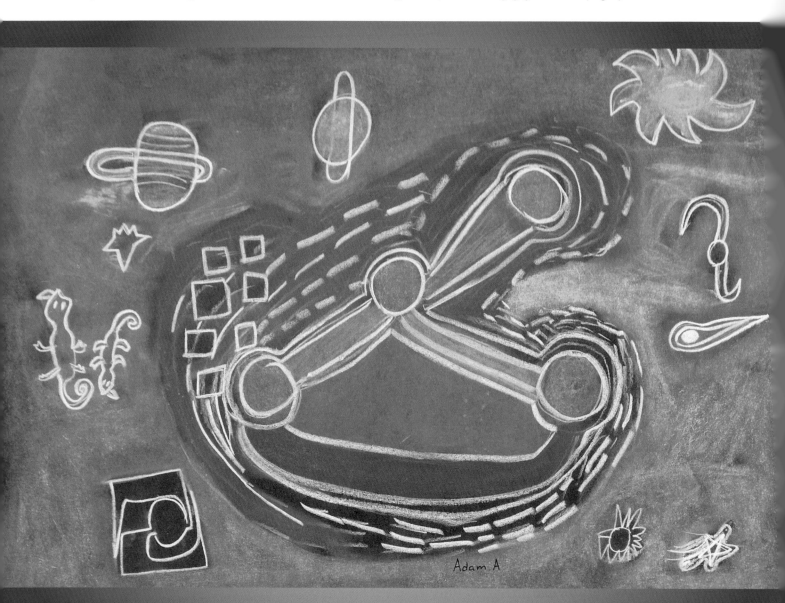

Adam A

How was the universe created?

There are different beliefs about how the universe was created. Some people believe that God created it. Others believe that spirits created it. However, the scientists believe that it all began with a 'Big Bang'.

They believe that first it was dark, and then there was a gigantic explosion and a huge flash of light. Scientists believe that the explosion happened around 13.7 billion years ago and that there was nothing before that.

This is when time began.

What happened after the 'Big Bang?'

The 'Big Bang' created a huge fireball. It was unimaginably hot. After less than a billion years the fireball cooled off and galaxies began to form.

What is a galaxy?

A galaxy is a huge family of stars that travels around in space. One of them is our galaxy named the Milky Way.

How many galaxies are there in the universe?

Scientists think that there may be more than 100 billion galaxies in the universe. Astronomers have been able to use telescopes to take photos of millions of them.

What do the galaxies look like?

Galaxies form in different shapes, the four most common shapes are: spiral, barred, elliptical and irregular galaxies.

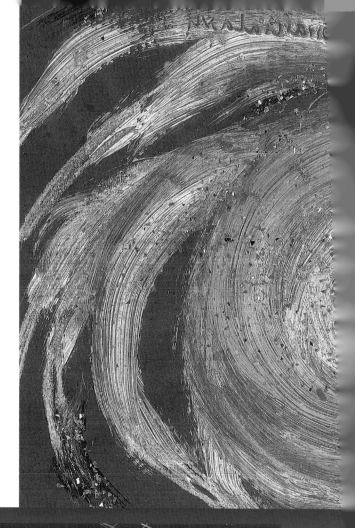

A spiral galaxy has a bright middle and two or more curved arms of stars.

A barred spiral galaxy has a central bar with an arm at each end.

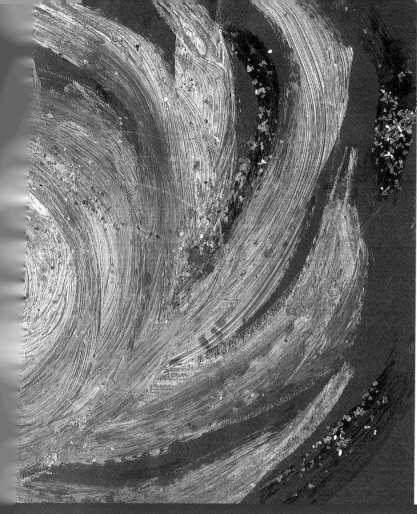

Which are the closest galaxies to the Milky Way?

The galaxies closest to our galaxy, the Milky Way, are the large and small Magellan Clouds. They are small, irregular galaxies. The second closest galaxy to our Milky Way is the Andromeda Galaxy. This is a large spiral galaxy.

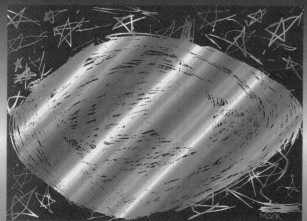

An elliptical galaxy has masses of old, red stars, which contain little gas or dust. Elliptical galaxies vary in shape from circular to oval.

An irregular galaxy doesn't have any fixed shape. They are just like clouds of stars.

What is a star?

A star is a ball of hot gas that produces heat and light that we see from Earth. Stars come in lots of different sizes. Their brightness varies.

What is a solar system?

A solar system is a collection of planets, asteroids and moons that travel around a Sun.

What's in our solar system?

Our solar system consists of a star, which is our Sun, eight planets and their moons, the Asteroid Belt, which lies between Mars and Jupiter, the Kuiper Belt which lies beyond Neptune, and five dwarf planets Ceres, Pluto, Haumea, Makemake and Eris.

Ceres is located in the Asteroid Belt, the other dwarf planets are found in the outer solar system.

What is the Asteroid Belt?

The Asteroid Belt is an area of space between Mars and Jupiter. Together with all the planets it orbits the Sun. The Asteroid Belt is made up of many millions of asteroids, some of them are very large and some are very small. The biggest asteroid is a dwarf planet called Ceres. It is about one-quarter the size of our Moon.

What is the Kuiper Belt?

The Kuiper Belt is an area of our solar system that exists beyond Neptune. Together with the planets it orbits the Sun. It is similar to the Asteroid Belt, but is made up of thousands and thousands of different sizes of icy bits and pieces. It is at least 20 times wider than the Asteroid Belt.

How did the planets get their names?

Before the invention of the telescope, people could only see some of the planets. They named them after Greek and Roman gods and goddesses. So Jupiter, Saturn, Mars, Venus and Mercury were given their names thousands of years ago.

In 1611, when Galileo invented the first telescope other planets were discovered and named after Greek and Roman gods or goddesses. Mercury was the Roman god of travel. Venus was the Roman goddess of love and beauty. Earth is an English and German name, which means the ground. Mars was the Roman god of war. Jupiter was the king of the Roman gods, and Saturn was the Roman god of agriculture. Uranus was an ancient Greek god of the sky. Neptune was the Roman god of the sea.

Venus

Venus is the second planet from the Sun. It is about the same size as the Earth. It is the hottest planet in our solar system. Venus spins in the opposite direction to the Earth. It takes 224.7 Earth days to orbit the Sun. Venus is one of the inner planets. It is made of rock. Venus has no moons.

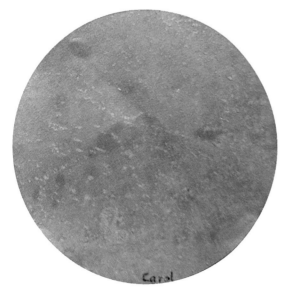

Mercury

Mercury is the closest planet to the Sun. It is the smallest planet in our solar system. Although it is the closest to the Sun, it is not the hottest planet. Mercury takes 88 Earth days to orbit the Sun. It travels faster than any other planet. Mercury is one of the inner planets. It is made of rock and metals. Mercury has no moons.

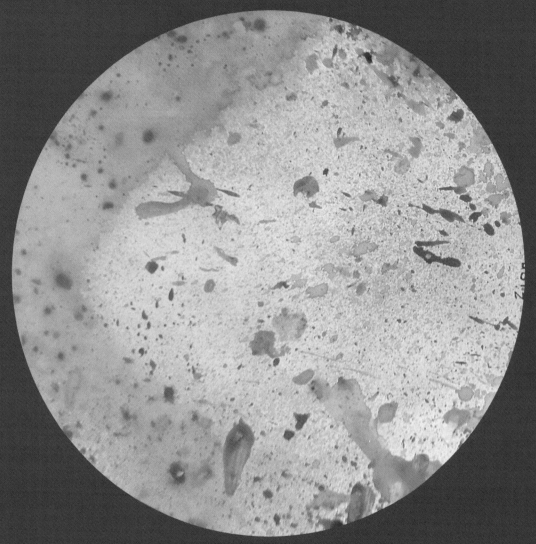

The Sun

The Sun is a star. It is a gigantic ball made of exploding gasses. It gives us light and warmth. Without the Sun there would be no life on Earth.

Earth

Earth is the third planet from the Sun. It is about the same size as Venus. Earth is the only planet that has liquid water on its surface and the only planet to have life. It takes 365 ¼ days to orbit the Sun, but the ¼ days are added up every four years. This is called a leap year and it has 366 days. A leap year is always a year with an even number, for example 2008, 2012 and 2016. While the Earth orbits round the Sun it turns on its axis, rotating right round in 24 hours. The side of the Earth that faces the Sun has daytime and the side of the Earth that is turned away from the Sun has night-time. When it is night time in Europe, it is daytime on the opposite side of the Earth in Australia.

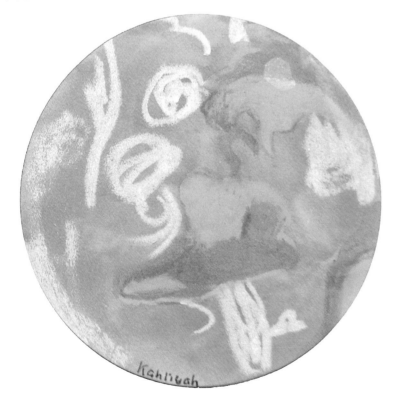

Kahliyah

EQUATOR

Tyson

As the Earth orbits round the Sun it tilts very slightly which makes the seasons. When the Earth is tilted so that the northern half of the Earth is a little away from the Sun, the northern hemisphere has winter. When the southern hemisphere is tilted very slightly towards the Sun the southern hemisphere has summer. Winter in Europe means summer in Australia. There is much less difference between summer and winter in countries close to the Equator. Earth is one of the inner planets. It has one Moon.

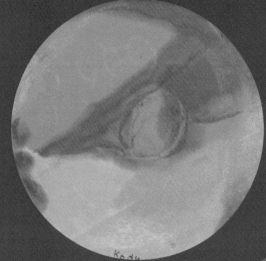

Mars

Mars is the fourth planet from the Sun. It is about half the size of Earth. It is a very cold planet. It takes Mars 25 hours to rotate once on its axis. It takes 868 Earth days to orbit the Sun. Because of the tilt it has seasons similar to the Earth. Mars is one of the inner planets. It is made of rock. Mars has two moons.

Jupiter

Jupiter is the fifth planet from the Sun. It is the biggest planet in our solar system, being one thousand times bigger than Earth. It takes 10 hours to rotate around its axis. It takes 12 Earth years to orbit the Sun. Jupiter is one of the outer planets. It is made of gasses such as hydrogen, helium, methane and ammonia. Jupiter has 67 moons.

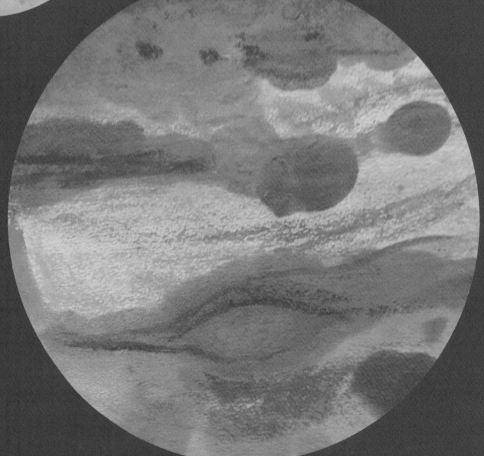

Saturn

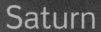

Saturn is the sixth planet from the Sun. It is the second largest planet in the solar system. It takes 10 hours to rotate on its axis. It takes 29 ½ years to orbit the Sun. Saturn is one of the outer planets. It is made of gas, mostly hydrogen. The rings around Saturn are made of dust and rocks. It has more than 60 moons.

Uranus

Uranus is the seventh planet from the Sun. It cannot be seen without a telescope. Uranus takes 17 hours and 54 minutes to rotate on its axis. It lies on its side orbiting the Sun, which take 84 Earth years. Uranus is one of the outer planets. It is made of gas. Most of the centre of Uranus is a frozen mass of ammonia and methane, which gives it a blue-green colour. It has 27 moons.

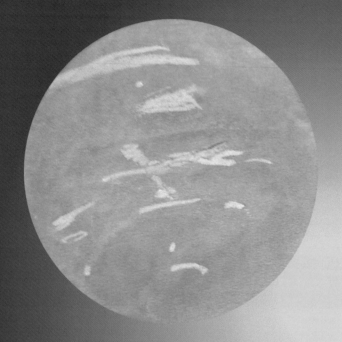

Neptune

Neptune is the eighth planet from the Sun. It cannot be seen without a telescope. It takes Neptune 16 hours to rotate on its axis. It takes 165 Earth years to orbit the Sun. Neptune is one of the outer planets. It is made of gas. It has 14 moons.

Planet 9

Two astronomers from America believe that there may be a ninth planet in our solar system. They believe that this gigantic planet is positioned beyond Neptune.

What keeps the planets in place?

The planets in our solar system are held in place by gravity. The Sun has the strongest gravity of all and the planets are forced to keep to their paths around it. Gravity is also what keeps a moon in place around its planet.

What are constellations?

Constellations are groups of stars that make imaginary shapes in the night sky. The different constellations are named after mythological figures, people, animals and objects. For thousands of years, people all over the world have made imaginary shapes out the same group of stars. The Europeans for example, made human and animal shapes such as a dog and humans such as Orion, a great hunter armed with a club and a shield, as he faces the big bull Taurus. In Australia Aboriginal people mostly made animal shapes. Wurrawana the Tasmanian Tiger, Tchingal the Emu and Barrukill the Kangaroo. These are some of the best known shapes.

The Dog Constellation

The Bear Constellation

The Orion Constellation

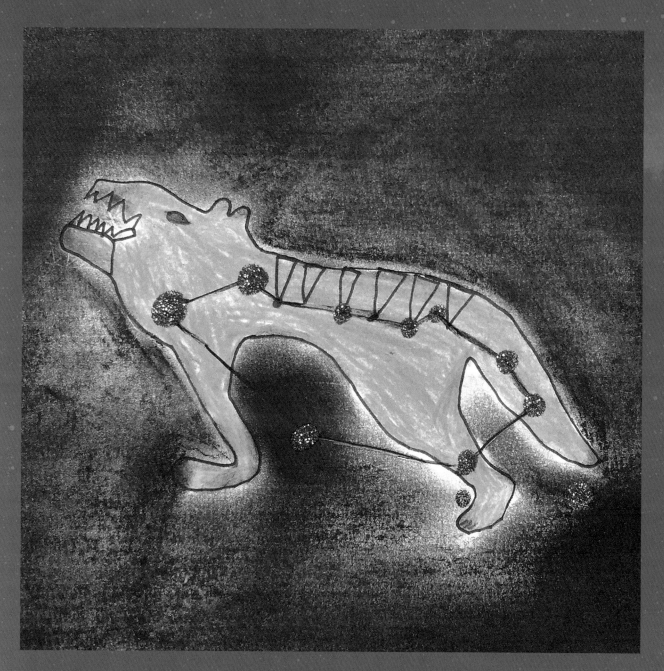

The Tasmanian Tiger Constellation

The Emu Constellation

The Kangaroo Constellation

Where did the first astronomers come from?

The Babylonians, Egyptians, Chinese and many other cultures around the world have also looked at the night sky and wondered how it all worked. Many cultures even believed that the world was a flat disk rather than a sphere. Aristotle, a Greek philosopher said that this was not true. "Earth" he said "is a sphere!"

Joseph

Tyren.

What did the ancient Greek astronomers discover?

Some clever people in ancient Greece began to wonder and ask questions. They wanted to find out more about the universe. They asked questions and discussed among themselves what the answers could be. They also tried to work out the best ways to find the answers.

Aristotle was born 384BCE in Greece. He was a famous philosopher and mathematician. He was among the first to use experiments to find answers. He developed logical ways of thinking.

Aristotle claimed that Earth was in the middle of our solar system, and the Sun and the other planets revolved around Earth. Because Aristotle was such a knowledgeable man and highly respected, no one thought he could be wrong. Aristotle died in 322BCE.

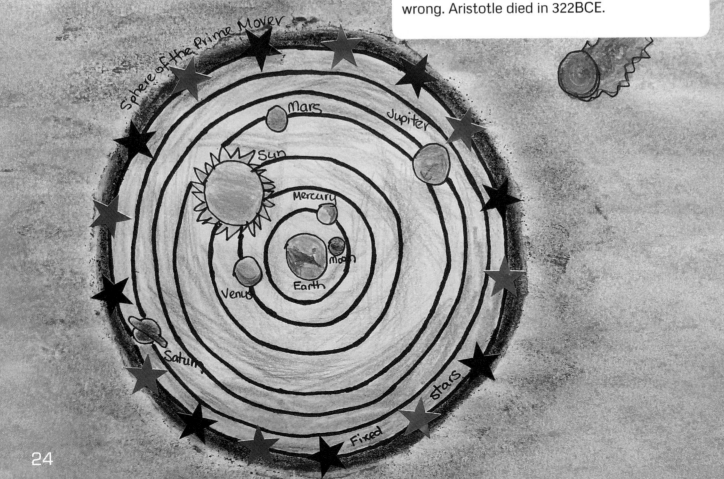

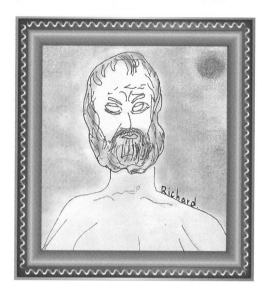

Aristarchus was born 310BCE on the Greek island of Samos. He was a mathematician and astronomer.

He thought that the Sun, not the Earth, was the fixed centre of the solar system, and that the Earth, and the planets, revolved around the Sun. He also said that the stars were far away suns that stayed in the same place and that the size of the universe was much bigger than anyone could imagine. Unfortunately Aristarchus could not prove his ideas. He died in 230BCE.

Claudius Ptolemy was born 90BCE in Alexandria, Egypt. He was a mathematician, astronomer, geographer, astrologer, poet and cartographer.

Ptolemy accepted Aristotle's idea that the Sun and the planets revolve around Earth. He developed this idea by observing the heavens. He was convinced that he was right, because he had worked it out mathematically. Ptolemy said that the Earth is in the centre of our solar system, and the Sun, stars and the planets revolve around Earth. He wrote the Almagest, which contained a list of stars and ways for positioning planets. He died in 168BCE.

What did astronomers of the modern world discover?

Nicolas Copernicus was born 1473CE in Poland. He was an astronomer and mathematician.

Copernicus agreed with Aristarchus that Earth and the other planets were orbiting the Sun. He was the first person to publish a book about this idea. The Roman Catholic Church banned the book. They didn't like the idea of the Sun being the centre of our solar system. Copernicus also worked out that the Earth rotates on its axis. This idea was difficult for most people to understand. Copernicus kept very quiet about his work, because he knew that the Church didn't like it, and they could easily have put him in jail. Copernicus' work was published shortly after his death in 1543CE.

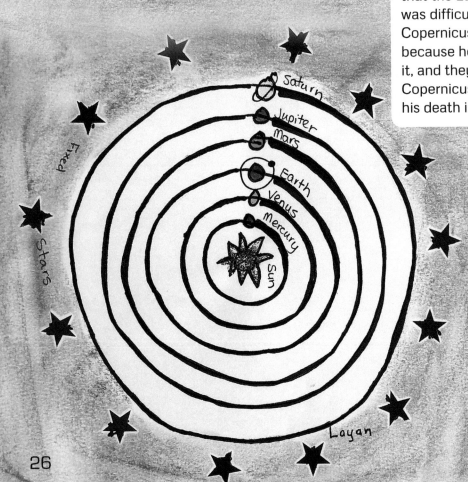

Tycho Brahe was born 1546CE in Denmark. He was an astronomer who was known for what was then thought to be an accurate and complete description of our solar system. He also discovered a super nova.

Tycho Brahe supported the idea that Earth was the centre of our solar system. However, he claimed that Venus and Mercury orbited the Sun and together with Mars, Jupiter and Saturn they all revolved around Earth.

The Danish King, Christian IV gave Tycho Brahe an island called Hven, where he built a planetarium so that he could study the stars. But Tycho was a greedy man who wanted more and more from the King. After many disagreements with the King about money, Tycho Brahe left Denmark. He was then invited by the Bohemian King Rudolph II to live in Prague, Czechoslovakia. In Prague Johannes Kepler was his assistant. Tycho Brahe died in 1601CE.

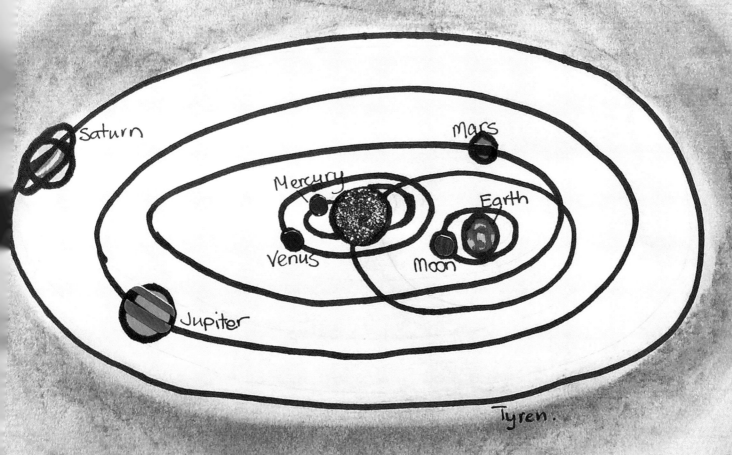

Johannes Kepler was born 1571CE in Germany. He studied mathematics, theology, philosophy and astronomy. Kepler moved to Prague, Czechoslovakia where he worked for Tycho Brahe. However, Kepler was a clever man. He disagreed with Tycho Brahe's model of our solar system and worked out that Copernicus' model, which shows that the Sun is in the centre of our solar system, was correct. He also worked out, using mathematics, that the orbit of the planets is an ellipse and not a circle. Kepler died in 1630CE.

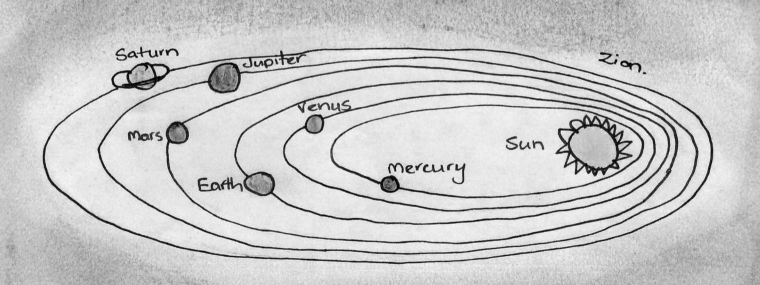

Galileo Galilee was born 1564CE in Pisa, Italy. He was a professor of mathematics at Pisa University. Galileo was the first astronomer to use what we call science to find out what the universe is made of.

Galileo discovered that mass does not affect gravitational pull. In theory, all things should fall at the same rate, regardless of how heavy they are. To prove his theory, Galileo is said to have dropped two cannonballs of different sizes from the Leaning Tower of Pisa to demonstrate that they would land on the ground at the same time.

In 1609, Galileo heard about a new invention, from Holland, called a spyglass which was used to spy on pirates. Galileo decided to improve the spyglass so it could be used to look at the universe. This spyglass was renamed the 'telescope' in 1611.

Galileo discovered that the Milky Way is made up of millions of stars, each at a different distance from the Earth. When he looked at the Moon he saw mountains, valleys and craters. Galileo discovered four moons around Jupiter. Galileo agreed with Copernicus' idea that the Sun is in the middle of our solar system. He published his observations and ideas. But he got in big trouble with the Catholic Church. He was taken to court, where he, out of fear for his life, decided to say that he was wrong. Galileo was kept under house arrest for the rest of his life. While under house arrest Galileo's famous book, about his observations, was smuggled out of Italy and published in Holland. He died in 1642CE.

Edmond Halley was born 1656CE in England. He was a mathematician and astronomer. In 1682 Halley saw a bright comet with a long brilliant sparkling tail.

Astronomers know that the Babylonians noticed this well-known object long before the time of Halley. However, he predicted that the comet would return 76 years later and when it did, it was named in his honour Halley's Comet. The last time it was visible was in 1986, and it is expected to return in 2061. Halley died in 1742CE.

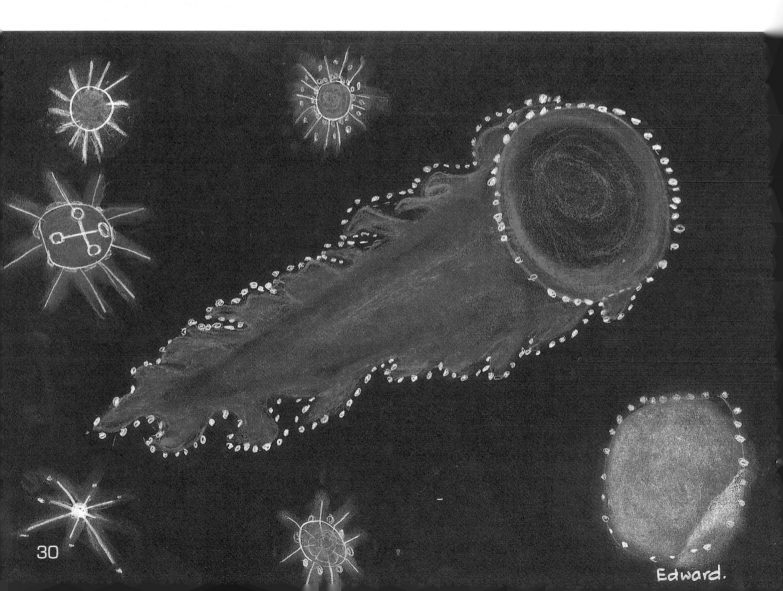

Edward.

Isaac Newton was born 1642CE in England. He was an alchemist, mathematician, scientist and philosopher. Newton published a famous book, which described his discovery about gravity. Newton learned about gravity when he was sitting under an apple tree and watched an apple falling to the ground. He realised there was a reason that the apple fell down to the ground instead of flying up in the air. Newton wrote many books about the law of gravity. In his third law, he said, "that for every action there is an equal and opposite reaction." He died in 1727CE.

How does Newton's third law work?

You can show this by making an experiment with a balloon. Blow it up, and see what happens when you let the air out of a balloon? The air goes one way and the balloon moves in the opposite direction. Rockets work in much the same way. This means that the rocket's action is to push down on the ground with the force of its powerful fuel filled engines. The reaction is that the ground pushes the rocket upwards with the same force. Rockets need a lot of fuel in order to overcome Earth's gravity. They have to reach a speed of 28,000 km per hour to enter orbit.

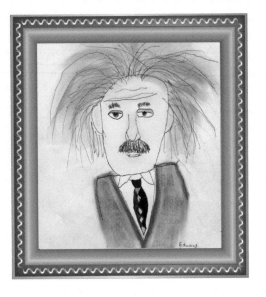

Albert Einstein was born 1879CE in Germany. He was a famous mathematician and physicist. Einstein was 16 years old when he worked out why the speed of light is always the same. (The speed of light is about 300.000 kilometres per second. It takes sunlight about 8 minutes to reach the Earth.) Einstein died in 1955CE.

Georges Lemaitre was born 1894CE in Belgium. He was an astronomer and a cosmologist. He was also a Catholic priest and a professor of astrophysics. Lemaitre discovered that the universe is expanding, getting bigger and bigger all the time. He said that because it is getting bigger, it must have started very small, with a 'Big Bang.' Lemaitre died in 1966CE.

Edwin Hubble was born 1889CE in Marsfield, USA. He studied mathematics, philosophy and astronomy. Hubble was able to demonstrate that other galaxies besides our own Milky Way existed. He also discovered that galaxies are moving away from one another, and that the universe is expanding. Hubble supported Lemaitre's idea of the 'Big Bang', which happened about 13.7 billion years ago. Hubble died in 1953CE.

What does the Hubble Space Telescope do?

In 1990 the world's first Space Telescope was launched. It was named the Hubble Space Telescope in honour of Edwin Hubble. Over the years the Hubble Space Telescope has sent new and valuable information back to Earth about distant planets, galaxies and other outer space objects. Since 1990 it has sent more than 1.2 million pictures back to Earth.

Will space research continue?

The work of the earlier scientists continues to this day. To learn more, we must ask questions, invent new instruments such as computers, telescopes, cameras and space vehicles. We must also look at science, mathematics and reasoning. Then we will continue to learn more about the fascinating history of our universe.

Important events in space exploration

1957 Russia, then called the Soviet Union, launched the first artificial satellite, named Sputnik 1, into space. Later the same year they launched Sputnik 2 carrying a dog, named Laika.

1959 The Soviet Union sent the first probe, Luna 2 to the Moon.

1961 The Soviet Union sent the first person Yuri Gagarin into space. The flight lasted less than two hours.

1962 The USA sent John Glenn to orbit the Earth in the Friendship 7 spacecraft. During the trip, Glenn flew over Perth and noticed that the people of Perth had turned on their lights to acknowledge his mission. Glen could clearly see Perth from space, so our city became known all over the world as the 'City of Lights'.

1963 The Soviet Union sent the first woman, Valentina Tereshkova, into space. The flight lasted for nearly three days.

1965 The USA sent the space probe, Mariner 4 into space to take pictures of Mars.

1966 The Soviet Union's space probe, Luna 9 was the first to land on the Moon.

1967 The Soviet Union's space probe, Venera 4 was the first to land on Venus.

1968 The USA sent three astronauts around the Moon in Apollo 8.

1969 The USA landed the first three men on the Moon. They were Neil Armstrong, Buzz Aldrin and Michael Collins. They landed in the lunar module named the 'Eagle'.

1969 Three months after Neil Armstrong, Buzz Aldrin and Michael Collins landed on the Moon, they paid a short visit to Perth. More than 50,000 people lined the streets to welcome and hail the famous astronauts.

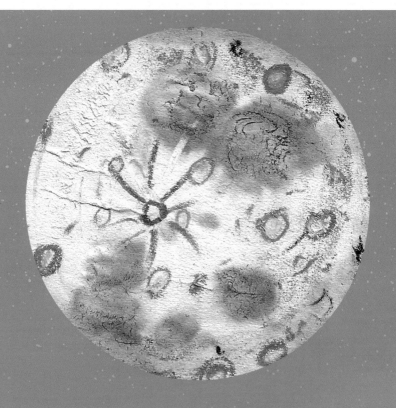

1971

The USA sent astronauts on the fourth, fifth and sixth Apollo missions to explore the Moon. They used a Moon car called the Lunar Rover. One of the astronauts David Scott made an experiment based on Galileo's discovery that mass does not affect gravitational pull, therefore all objects, no matter their size will fall and hit the ground at the same time.

While he was on the Moon, Scott dropped a feather and a hammer at the same time, and as Galileo had found many years ago, both the feather and the hammer hit the ground at the same time. On Earth the experiment would have turned out a little different because Earth's atmosphere would cause the feather to drop slower.

Atmosphere is the air that all living things breathe to survive. It is mostly made up of nitrogen and oxygen. As there is no atmosphere in space, astronauts need to bring large amounts of oxygen with them when they travel in space. Most people can only survive a few minutes without oxygen.

Fire is another thing that needs oxygen. You can find out by making an experiment with tea candles. Take two Tea candles and a glass jar. Light the candles and cover one of the candles with the glass jar. After a while the flame will die. Why? Because fire need oxygen and when the glass jar covers the candle, oxygen can't reach the flame and when the oxygen inside the jar is used up the flame goes out. Without oxygen no living things will survive.

1976 The USA's space probes Viking 1 and Viking 2 landed on Mars.

1990 The Hubble space telescope was launched.

2000 The International Space Station was launched. Astronauts can live on this space station as they make experiments and test spacecraft instruments.

2000 The first permanent crew moved into the international space station.

2004 Spaceship One was launched with three private passengers. This was the first time ordinary people went into space.

2030s
Scientists are planning to send people to Mars.

How else have people explained the mysteries of the universe?

For thousands of years people have been
aware of the mysteries of the universe.
The movement of the stars, night and day,
the seasons and eclipses were studied and
explained through art and storytelling

Australian Aboriginal Astronomy

Australian Aboriginal people are probably the world's oldest known astronomers. They studied the night sky carefully and worked out how constellations, planets and the stars move. They also worked out that the Moon controls the tide and that eclipses happen when the paths of the Sun and Moon cross one another.

The Noongar people, of south Western Australia, followed a calendar of six seasons instead of the four season calendar of summer, autumn, winter and spring. The six seasons are named Birak, Bunuru, Djeran, Makuru, Djiba, and Kambarang. Birak is the first summer of the months December and January. During this time an afternoon breeze cools the warm days. Bunuru is the second summer of the months of February and March. At this time there is very little rain. Djeran is autumn running from April to May. Makuru runs from June to July. This is the time when the first rain begins to fall.

Djilba runs from August to September. This is the time of the second rains. Kambarang runs from October to November. With each season, the Noongar people would eat what they could find while they walked from place to place. So as you can see astronomy helped them in their daily living.

The followering Dreamtime stories have been told by different tribes around Australia. Two stories explain why we have night and day and two explain the constellations.

The Dreamtime story of The Sun

Retold by students, Room 4 from Wuriunpranli, The Sun Woman.

Once there was a special woman by the name Wuriunpranli. She had a blazing torch made of a stringy bark tree. The torch was the Sun that gives us light and warmth.

Every morning while it was still very dark Wuriunpranli would light a little fire which became dawn. Dawn is the part of the day when the Sun comes up. Wuriunpranli always made herself pretty by painting her body and face with red ochre powder. The ochre powder often flew into the sky and clouds where it made a beautiful red sunrise. As the Sun was rising the birds sang to wake up all the people on Earth.

Wuriunpranli used the flames from the campfire to light her giant torch. Every day she would travel across the sky, making the long journey from the east, to the night camp site on the west. Her blazing torch lit up the whole world so that people and animals could find food to eat.

As she reached the west, disappearing over the horizon, she stopped and turned down her flaming torch so that it gave only very little light and heat. Again she decorated herself with red ochre which made a beautiful red sunset.

Every evening she entered a deep long tunnel that she walked through to get back to the morning camp. At sunset all the birds would go to sleep in the trees. Every morning when Wuriunpranli lit her torch, they sang to wake up all the people on Earth.

The Dreamtime story of The Moon

Retold by students, Room 4 from Origins of The Moon

This is the story of how the Moon got into the sky.

A long time ago there was no Moon and no light after the Sun had gone down. People could only smell, hear and feel things, but they couldn't see anything. They couldn't walk around because they were scared of bumping into things surrounding them. The darkness felt like it was pushing them down with its weight, so they bent over. This was not easy, especially when they had to dance at the corroborees. They kept bumping into each other .

Then one night one of the dancers saw a faint light coming towards them. He was very surprised. He stopped dancing and told the others to look too. When the light came closer, they could see a strange looking youth carrying the light in a dilly bag.

They said to the youth, "welcome to our camp! Can we have your bag with the light? We will give you anything you want in exchange!"

"OK" said the youth, 'but you will have to give me a wife and shelter!" The people agreed to give the youth what he asked for.

The next morning the people took the bag with the light. They looked at it, turned it upside down and even poked it with sticks. But there was no light at all, so there was nothing special about the bag. The people got angry, because they thought they had been tricked. They began to make a plan to have revenge on the youth. They thought about a corroboree that would give them mighty power over him. But the youth surprised the people by interrupting the corroboree. He saw the dilly bag on the ground, so he picked it up and opened it. To everyones surprise, a bright light came out of the bag.

"We want that bag! That one has the light in it!" everyone yelled.

"It's the same bag", said the youth.

"No it's not, you tricked us, the light was not in the other bag!" said the people.

"It's the same bag!" the youth argued.

"The light won't work during the day because the Sun has such powerful light you can't see the special light in this bag."

The youth was mad with the people because they had accused him of cheating. So he took the bag with the light from the people and threw it into the night sky so that everyone on Earth could see it. That's how our Moon got into the sky.

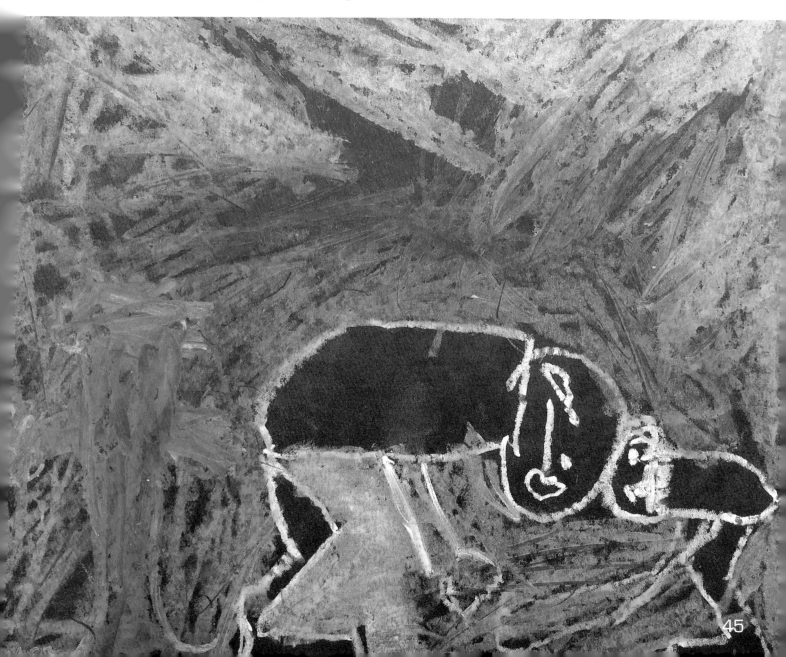

The Noongar Dreamtime story of the Southern Cross

Retold by students, Room 4 from Koodjal-Koodjal Djookan The Legend of the Southern Cross.

Once in the Dreamtime there were four Noongar women who lived next to the sea. They had set up a camp near a forest full of huge trees.

The local river, where they would get their water from, was far away. The elders of the tribe realised that they would soon run out of water. So the elders sent the four women with cups made of bark to get water to the tribe. The elders told the women that they were forbidden to go near the waterhole, which was only for men.

The women disobeyed the elders and went to the sacred waterhole. Their curiosity made them disobey the elders. Once they had filled up their cups they happily danced around the waterhole.

The men thought, "what is taking the women so long?" So they set out to find them. They searched the river, but they were not there. As the men were walking away, they heard talking and laughing coming from the sacred waterhole. When the men discovered the women were at the forbidden waterhole, they were furious.

Suddenly the women saw the men coming towards them with spears. So they ran away as fast as they could. But… as they were running, a strange, powerful wind blew them up into the sky. The women huddled together, and as such, became a very easy target, for the angry men, to spear. The women quickly spread out into a cross pattern so the angry men couldn't spear them easily.

This became known as the constellation named the Southern Cross. We can still see the brightest stars that make up the Southern Cross because of the four women who were too afraid to come back to Earth.

Kahliyah

The Dreamtime story of the Seven Sisters.

Retold by students, Room 4 from The Legend of the Seven Sisters by May L O'Brien.

When we look up into the night sky we can see many twinkling stars. Some of the stars are grouped together, these are known as constellations, and they all have special names. One of them is called the Seven Sisters, also known as the Pleiades and this is their story.

A long time ago when only Aboriginal people lived in Australia there were very small men called Yayarrs. The Yayarrs walked all over the country. But every now and then they would leave Earth and travel to faraway places in the Milky Way, our own galaxy. When they came back to Earth they would land on their favourite hill.

The Seven Sisters also liked to visit Earth, and their favourite landing place was the same as the Yayarrs. One day the Sisters were just about to land, but the Yayarrs were on their special landing hill. The sisters called to the Yayarr men to move, but the Yayarrs refused to listen, so the Seven Sisters had to find another hill to land on.

The Yayarrs who were watching the Sisters, thought that they had the most beautiful hair. One of the men said, "let's follow them!" They all agreed.

Another man said, "let's marry them! Wait here, I'll catch them all by myself." He made sure that he didn't step on any sticks because that would have made noises. He waited patiently until one of the Sisters left the group. She was thirsty and went to look for water. Although the Yayarr man had been very careful not to be seen or heard, the Sister did see him. She ran as fast as she could, but the little Yayarr was too fast for her, he grabbed her as she was trying to escape.

The two struggled for a long time, then the Yayarr man tried to hit her with a big stick, but every time he missed and instead he hit a rock. While he was hitting the rock the Sister ran towards the hill where the Seven Sisters had landed on Earth. In the distance she could hear the Yayarr man's voice calling after her.

When she got to the hill she climbed up the side. By the time she reached the top she was gasping for breath. She looked around for her sisters, but she could tell by the shadow that she was too late, Her sisters had returned to the sky. She felt very sad and lonely. After a while she stopped crying, she looked up into the sky and she could see all of her sisters. She decided to leave Earth so that the Seven Sisters could be united once again.

This is the constellation known as the Seven Sisters or the Pleiades.

Bibliography

Bone, E. and Pastor, T. *The Solar System*. London: Usborne Publishing, 2010.

Brasch, N. *Sky Watching*. Melbourne: Thompson Learning Australia, 2004.

Brennan, B. *Aboriginal astronomers: world oldest?* Australian Geographic. 97, Jan–Mar 2010: 68.

D'Arcy, P. *The Emu in the Sky. Stories about the Aboriginals and the day and night skies*. (Canberra): The National Science and Technology Centre, (nd).

D'Arcy, P. *The Hunter in the Sky. Stories about the Aboriginals and the day and night skies*. (Canberra): The National Science and Technology Centre, 1997.

Hassell, Ethel and Davidson, D.S. *Myths and Folktales of the Wheelman Tribe of South-Western Australia*. London: Taylor and Francis Ltd., 1934.

Jeunesse, G., et al. *The Universe*. Sydney: Scholastic Inc., 2005.

Miles, Lisa and Smith, Alastair. *The Usborne Internet – Linked Book of Astronomy & Space*. London: Usborne Publishing, 2001.

Norris, R. and Norris C. *Emu Dreaming An Introduction to Australian Aboriginal Astronomy*. Sydney: Emu Dreaming, 2009.

O'Brian, M. L. *The Legend of the Seven Sisters. A Traditional Aboriginal Story from Western Australia*. Canberra: Aboriginal Studies Press, 1990.

Patston, G. et al. *Aboriginal Sky Figures*. Sydney: Australian Broadcasting Corporation, 1996.

Petterson, C. *Koodjal-Koodjal Djookan. The Legend of the Southern Cross. Using knowledge of the Noongar Minung –Gnudju people*. Batchelor (NT): Batchelorpress, 2007.

Websites

biography.com
www.emudreaming com
www.nasa.gov
space.com
www.spacekids.co.uk
universetoday.com
http://museum.wa.gov.au/city-lights
en.wikipedia.org

Thank you

We the Year Twos and Threes wish to thank all the wonderful people who have wholeheartedly supported us in this exciting, and sometimes difficult journey in writing a book about the fascinating history of astronomy.

Our classroom teacher, Mrs Lis Mathiasen, for her enthusiastic and explicit teaching of astronomy. We are grateful for the way she guided us through the many hours spent writing pages about astronomy, to produce our own publication. By doing so, science, Aboriginal studies, geography, mathematics, arts and reading and writing became interesting and exciting. Mrs Mathiasen, a gifted writer herself, has written several educational publications. She has recently published a retelling of a Hans Christian Andersen book for children, titled *It's Quite True*.

Mrs Tammy Loo, Indigenous Para Professional, for her constant encouragement, strong support and patience that she so generously gave to every student, during their journey in becoming an illustrator and an author of dreamtime astronomy stories. Mrs Loo is passionate about education and getting children to think outside the box. She finds childrens' creativity, tenacity and humour uplifting. Mrs Loo has supported numerous children in their zest to produce outstanding artwork using different media. Mrs Loo illustrated *What's Inside Me?* a book for children published in 2013.

Mrs Adeline Ryder, Indigenous Para Professional and Co-ordinator for the Aboriginal Playgroup, for her ongoing interest, encouragement and strong support in this important project. Mrs Ryder is passionate about young children's health and well-being and has won several awards for outstanding community work.

Ms Mandy Cheetham, a former senior public Librarian and currently a volunteer at Westminster Junior Primary School, for her enthusiastic interest and support in proof reading and editing our work. Ms Cheetham has experience in editing fiction and non-fiction manuscripts. She has a particular interest in history, astronomy and children's literature. Ms Cheetham is also passionate about supporting young children in their aspirations to become authors and illustrators.

Mr Mathiasen, former social worker, who has generously supported our book project. The support of Mr Mathiasen has played a key role in the success of this important project being published. Mr Mathiasen is a humanitarian and a philanthropist. Over the years, he has donated his time and funds to several charitable causes.

Mrs Cynthia Mathew, accredited provider of Reading For Sure - The Solomon Method, in private practice, for her generous donation towards our publication. Mrs Mathew strongly believes that every child is able to become literate. Her passion and tenacity has assisted numerous children in overcoming literacy difficulties and achieve wonderful results. Mrs Mathew is a philanthropist. She has donated ongoing funds to several charitable causes.

Mrs Judith Price, author, illustrator and graphic artist, for the time and effort she has taken to design and set up our book. She has produced an outstanding publication that makes us feels very proud of our work. Mrs Price has recently illustrated and published a retelling of Hans Christian Andersen's story titled *It's Quite True*.

The Astronomy project was initiated in the beginning of the year by the students' relentless interest in space. As such, this project became an integrated differentiated curriculum covering the required content of science, Aboriginal studies, geography, arts and literacy. Throughout the year, students have collaboratively and enthusiastically made decisions, researched, conducted experiments, discussed outcomes, written science reports and produced outstanding artwork. They have also structured and edited fiction and non-fiction writing. This process has concluded by the students producing their very own history of astronomy.

CPSIA information can be obtained at www.ICGtesting.com
Printed in the USA
LVIW01n1913131216
517094LV00007B/48